W9-BRI-906

Rubber Houses

a novel by *Ellen Yeomans*

LITTLE, BROWN AND COMPANY
New York ❧ Boston ❧ London

Little, Brown and Company

Hachette Book Group USA
1271 Avenue of the Americas, New York, NY 10020
Visit our Web site at www.lb-teens.com

First Edition: January 2007

AAA is a registered trademark of American Automobile
Association, Inc.

Library of Congress Cataloging-in-Publication Data
Yeomans, Ellen, 1962–
Rubber houses / by Ellen Yeomans. — 1st ed.
p.   cm.
Summary: A novel in verse that relates seventeen-year-old Kit's
experiences as her younger brother is diagnosed with and dies of cancer
and as she withdraws into and gradually emerges from her grief.
ISBN-13: 978-0-316-10647-4 (hardcover)
ISBN-10: 0-316-10647-X (hardcover)
[1. Grief—Fiction.   2. Death—Fiction.   3. Brothers and sisters—
Fiction.   4. Family life—Fiction.]   I. Title.
PZ7.Y425Rub 2007
[Fic]—dc22   2005037297

10 9 8 7 6 5 4 3 2 1

Q-FF

Printed in the United States of America

The text was set in Perpetua, and the display type is Silvermoon.

FOR CHRISARNOLD

MY BOY WITH A BROOM

Warm-Ups

Second week of April, Junior year

ANTICIPATION

This is the summer
Callie and I
are going to fly

Gas up my car
day-trip our way across the state
or at least as far
as our paychecks will take us
and our parents will allow us

We're both going to get good jobs
with weekends off
cute guys all around
maybe at the village pool
or parks and rec
plenty of rays, plenty of pay, plenty of play

We'll make memories
we'll make secrets
we'll make coded references
beneath our senior pictures
on our yearbook page

This is the summer
Callie and I
are going to fly

Wrong Latitude

Trudge through
slush like this and snow like that
with the usual Thursday homework load
that comes of taking too many AP courses and
caring too much about them and wishing
spring would just get here finally up the
walkway and to the side door managing not to
slip where the ice builds up from the snow and
thaw and snow and thaw that fall-winter-spring
keeps delivering
finally in the door,
finally in the warm kitchen,
finally home and then I
slip on what must be my brother's spare pair of
    snow pants,
crash to the wooden floor sending all those
    books
skating across the kitchen to
finally slam against the refrigerator
as I sprawl on that wooden floor
butt-bruised and brain-busted
wondering why on earth my parents
decided on Here
when there are places called Florida and
    California,
South Carolina and Texas,
all which could have been
called Home.

Snow Ball

Flash of red chest protector
against white drifts,
dark snowsuits, ball cap beaks,
they look like the robins we ought to have
   around by now.
Buddy's out there catching whatever Aziz can
   throw,
winter gloves crammed inside mitts
two nine-year-olds
willing their favorite season, baseball, to begin.
Pop flies then grounders
lost in knee-high snow,
they search, they find and
they might just bring spring in.

CABIN FEVER

Can't remember
when I didn't
look up driving distances,
study routes and destinations
longitude, latitude, topography,
legends and keys,
a world waiting for me
on paper
to plot, to estimate, to travel.

When I was thirteen
I redecorated my room.
Painted it blue and green,
papered a whole wall with
maps from *National Geographic*
and Triple A.

Not many pins
stuck in to show where I've been,
but I've got plans
and four different globes,
a beat-up stick-shifting Civic
and a feel for the back road.
I am so ready to leave.
On paper.

Scouting Report

Looking again from the warm side of the
  kitchen window,
I notice Buddy is throwing kinda funny, but I've
  seen it before,
Last week I guess.
Wonder if the snowsuit is too bulky or if he's
  just tired again?
And then they're in,
and I can't resist teasing
You losing your form, catcher boy? Having trouble
finding the mound?
I help him pull off his boots.
Naw, Aziz is just throwing heat, he says,
and now I'm too hot. Aziz you must be burning up,
  he calls out.
Buddy laughs at his own terrible joke,
hugs me before Aziz notices, and skates
by in his socks toward the teakettle.
I can't resist one more:
Better hope the Yankees weren't
scouting today.
He turns and flashes a sign that isn't any
  catcher's signal.
His face turns red as he realizes what he's just
  done and
all I can do is laugh and wonder how I
hadn't noticed my baby brother isn't such a
  baby anymore.

HOST

Their boots leaving puddles
near the back door,
at the counter, Buddy teaching Aziz
some camp song about rising and shining.
Buddy's looking pale but singing loudly,
his damp hair sticking straight up
on one side, his scarf still around his neck.
Making hot chocolate, Kit,
want some? I saved your favorite mug just in case.
Aziz swivels on his stool taking
what Buddy has to give
microwave beeping
hot milk spilt
chocolate powder grit
ground on the counter.
In his efforts, in his care,
Buddy seems to offer us a piece of himself,
along with a mug and a graham cracker.

WHAT IF I TRIED

and let go just a little,
stayed in this
warm kitchen, ate another cracker,
sipped more cocoa,
ignored my homework,
just for a night?
What if I tried
and let go just a little,
forgot my GPA, my class rank,
popped some corn?
What if I tried
and let go just a little,
read a magazine,
soaked in the tub,
worried less about the future,
took care of just now?
What if I tried to defy my nature?
Would the world stop spinning?
What if I tried, just for a night?

NOTHING

She sends Aziz home and hustles
Buddy toward the bathtub, flannel pj's, and bed.
Mom sure loves her schedules.
You stayed out in the snow too long, you're exhausted
  again.
Let's get going young man.

Hours later, my English essay and calculus
done, passing by their closed bedroom door
I can still hear Dad ask
Can little guys get mono? Do you think he has mono?
Mom sighs loudly enough for me to hear
His appointment is Monday, I'm sure it's nothing.
  It has to be nothing.
They didn't ask me, but if they did, would
  I agree
it's nothing?

SHOTGUN

I call shotgun, Buddy yells as
he races to his side of my car.
It's just the two of us,
who else is gonna ride shotgun?
I try to explain this expression to him as
we drive. He nods, smiles and
sings along with the radio, messing up the lyrics
    again
singing way too loud again, the Buddy Way.

I pull up at Dad's work site and
Buddy grabs the paper sack.
I bet Dad forgets his lunches on purpose
just to see us on Saturdays.
I'd be ticked off if I had plans
or if it didn't seem so sweet.
Dad hugs me, thanks me, then grabs
Buddy's hands and whirls him around
feet off the ground like a ride at the fair.
You're getting too old for this Budman, or
maybe it's me, Dad says, slowing the spin.
Back on land Buddy's giggling,
dizzy, begging for more.
One more twirl, one more hug
and he has to get back to work.
And it's time to get our Saturday
    ice cream cone.
Can we just go home instead, Kit? I guess I'm
    still full.

This is a first. He heads to the car.
Shotgun he calls again, not as loud.
The car door slams,
bang.

THE FAMILY OBSESSION

You know it's my fault really
this baseball fanaticism of his.
Sure, we spent those Sunday afternoon
home-game days at the ballpark
watching our Triple-A team take on all comers.
But even so, at first, for Buddy and me
it was about the hot dogs and foot stomps,
hot peanuts and seventh-inning stretch
and the sense of having Mom and Dad
relaxed, really *with* the two of us
yet somehow the two of them
giddy, romantic, dating,
away from all the stuff
they always said needed to get done
in the house
with the bills, around the yard.
That was what baseball did for us. And then
one day, after he had started T-ball
I showed Buddy the math of baseball
the statistics, how to keep score
a long fly to center with a runner on second
    thrown out at third
is an 8 to 5
a few numbers telling a story of a 9-inning
    game
simple, elegant, perfect
And it all came together in that brain of his
till baseball was more than family time,
more than a sport,

it's become
the frame of his little-boy life,
the core of his dreams,
his love,
our focus.

"Regular" Season

April–September

OPENING DAY

Perfect blue
cloudless sky.
Can't get bad news
on a day like this.

4TH PERIOD, CALCULUS

Callie and I
glancing at the clock,
10:05 . . . 10:09 . . . 10:18
glancing at each other,
wondering if it's
a good thing
I haven't been called
to the office.
Does it mean
Buddy's tests show
all is well
or are they only just beginning
to know
why my brother
bruises so easily,
sleeps so much,
doesn't play anymore
with the rest of the neighborhood
renegades?
I calculate
the time that might have passed
to stop at the pediatrician's,
pick up records,
drive to University General
for testing,
wait,
I suppose,
for results.

Callie is sure it's nothing
But I'm better with numbers
and don't like the
way this is all adding up.

LINE DRIVE

Callie's dad drives eighty miles an hour down
  Route 81
Taking me to University General
Is my brother dying?

God no, Kit. God no. I didn't realize. God.
Sorry. Too fast. He's stable.
Your mom said he was stable.
A transfusion. That's all. He's stable.

Callie's dad slows way down on Route 81
just to prove it.
A pickup blares to say too slow,
Is Buddy in the emergency room?

No. Intensive care.
Your mom didn't want you to drive yourself,
asked me to bring you up to Intensive care.
Third floor. I can walk you up there.
But only family can stay.

Callie's dad pulls off Route 81
And turns the wrong way on Emerson Avenue
makes an illegal "U" and drives
into the hospital circle.

It's okay, Mr. Parsons,
I can go on up
alone.

At the door
I turn to see
Callie's dad drive eighty miles an hour toward
  Route 81.

3RD FLOOR, INTENSIVE CARE

Push a giant button
on a pastel wall.
Doors slowly swing open
admitting me to a cave:
dark, quiet,
lights blink,
monitors beep.

Buddy's comic-book brain
would imagine this the Batcave
would pretend to drive the Batmobile
would make a cape from that sheet,

POW! WHAM! KAZOWIE! SLAM!

if he weren't lying there
attached by tubes
to beeping monitors and blinking lights.

DESTINATION

Back when
I just had my learner's permit
Buddy bugged me to test,
Get your license soon, Kit.
We'll go places, just me and you.
His skinny seven-year-old self
all fidgety and determined.
Where to Buddy?
What kind of adventure
do you think Mom is going to let us take?
It sprang from his lips,
Yankee Stadium,
we'll take a picnic and go.
Aw Buddy, no.
I hear it's crazy in New York
the cabs, the traffic.
We can't drive to New York,
not just me and you.
We'll all go someday,
Mom and Dad driving.
He nodded and smiled
not disappointed
like he knew a secret.

REMEMBER

Six months ago
that first day
brand-new license in hand,
Buddy ready for adventure.
We drove all the way to the Dippity Dip stand
custard twists and french fries
a blue-sky orange-leafed October day
in his big sister's ratty old-new car.
He wasn't at Yankee Stadium
licking that cone,
but he sure looked like
he was in heaven.

Signals

Buddy knows pop flies and batting order.
Buddy knows bunting and catcher's signals.
Buddy's not old enough
to know chemo,
to know cancer.
Do we explain
this new sport
new rules
new uniform
or wait till
he takes the field?

Hurry

Aziz pedals up our driveway
with a card and M&M's
Can you bring these to the hospital?
Dark eyes and damp lashes
looking anywhere but at me.
I take his offering,
He's out of intensive care, Aziz.
I could drive you up if it's okay with your mom.
He adjusts his helmet low over his eyes,
He's gonna be okay, right, Kit?
eyes on me at last.

Yeah, he's going to be okay, I say too fast.

Okay, good. Tell Buddy I got a new helmet,
we can bike down the Armand Hill Trail
when he gets back home.

He pedals away
before I can say
okay or
wait a minute or
I shouldn't be making promises.

Some Game

At first
he thought it was a game
Round of Chemo
like merry-go-
Round of Chemo
like ring-a-
Round of Chemo

When he found out
it meant another
round of needles,
round of throw up,
round of mouth sores,
he asked for
a new game.
But they couldn't stop.
Two more
rounds
might win the game.

EACH FRIDAY

Stop by his school.
Pick up assignments.
Protect his teacher from the truth.

Mrs. Sheehan expects
good reports, good progress,
a miracle.

Help her to believe.
Research is leading the way, Kit.
Nod.
They cure most pediatric cancers.
Nod.
Buddy is going to be just fine.
Nod.
You tell Buddy to get this work done
so he can start fifth grade
with his classmates come fall.

She nods crisply and smiles.
Smile back.
Another Friday exam passed.

ROUTINE

Tuesdays and Fridays are hospital days.
Mom and Dad take turns taking him
for chemo and platelets
for weigh-ins and blood tests.

Funny how fast this all makes sense,
how soon this feels like the way it's always been.

Mr. Social comes home after treatments,
Gotta new joke for ya, Kit.
Didja hear the one about the nurse and the bedpans?
just like every other day of his life.
Except he's throwing up every few hours,
crashed on the couch,
sleeping through Yankee games,
waiting for normal to return.

Funny how fast this all makes sense.

Until the tests come back today.
The treatments aren't working.

APPREHENSION

This was the summer
Callie and I
were going to fly

Gas up my car
day-trip our way across the state
or at least as far
as our paychecks could take us
and our parents would allow us

We were both going to get good jobs
with weekends off
cute guys all around
maybe at the village pool
or parks and rec
plenty of rays, plenty of pay, plenty of play

We would have made memories
we would have made secrets
we would have made coded references
beneath our senior pictures
on our yearbook page

This was the summer
Callie and I
were going to fly

Since First Grade

Callie and me
we've got our way.
She talks, I listen.
She has a crush, I conspire.
She breaks a heart, I consult.
She has enough pain, drama, hysteria,
for the two of us.
I have the reasoning, the salve, the big picture
for the both of us.

We are not equipped for role reversal.

Guidance Counselor

My parents?
They're fine.
My brother?
He'll be fine.
Thought I was here to talk about my SATs
and my AP grades,
which schools I was thinking of visiting this
    summer,
where I might apply.
I'm not going to talk about my feelings
You've got the wrong girl here.

See you again next week?
Fine.

DESTINATION II

I drive over to Triple A
to pick up the TripTik
to Boston.
Doesn't seem right
to order one up

for this.

We should be planning
a summer vacation,
campus visits,
even a day trip
in the Adirondacks —

not this.

At the counter,
I order another from the peppy lady
and pick up a travel guide too:
New York City.
For when he's better

than this.

TripTik

Must have been sixth grade
when I did that report
The History of Turnpikes and
Interstate Route System.
Couldn't have been happier
when I discovered the TripTik,
that spiral-bound set of maps
made to order
for your next trip,
American Automobile Association's
gift to the traveler.
I told my parents that's what I
would go to college for,
to become a TripTik Giver.
Dad laughed,
Mom suggested I set my sights higher
than a clerk at Triple A
explaining the science and art of mapmaking,
recommending a career in cartography.
I've since given up that career goal,
along with ballerina, cowgirl, astronaut.
And I know a few more things about maps:
the mapmaker is a good thing, a necessary
    thing,
but the map giver is
who you need when you're
looking for direction.

June 9

Buddy doesn't want to leave
Dr. Delaney's questions about movies that
    Buddy never sees,
Dr. Delaney's ribbing about the Yankees,
Dr. Delaney's jokes and his quiet, happy hope.
Buddy likes *our* hospital just fine.
He likes the mint chocolate chip ice cream
    sandwiches
Dr. Susan stops by with.
He likes his nurses, the stickers and the
    attention.

I don't want to leave
Callie and our plans
for swimming, sunning,
scoping hot guys.
I like my summers to be
sleeping till ten then rushing through chores.
Hooking up at the reservoir, a little thirsty,
    a little burned.
I like my summers to be about me.

But we have to leave.
Have to travel to that children's hospital,
have done what only they can do.
So Buddy can have mint chocolate chip
    ice cream sandwiches
reservoir summers someday,
and a chance at fifth grade.

OVER THE PLATE

Mom pulls out a chair for me
at the kitchen table,
Kit, I'm worried about you,
how all this is affecting you,
I think we should talk.
I do not want to get into this
with her,
Mom I have to study for finals
and I'm supposed to catch up with Callie and —
Mom eyes me like one of her projects
and pushes a plate of gingersnaps my way,
Sweetie, this must be stressful for you too.
You can talk to me.
But we never talk
about anything trickier than
schedules and schoolwork.
How are we going to talk about
life and death?
We'd need to have practiced just getting the ball
over the plate,
before we can handle anything
low and inside.

POTHOLE

Dad and I go for a drive
How you doing Kiddo
with all that's going on?
He pulls out.
You too, Dad? I'm fine. Really.
He turns.
Dad, you ought to take Douglas Street at this time
 of day.
Oh, yeah right. He takes the next left.
Kiddo, we need to be honest.
He signals.
Have you talked with your mother?
He swerves.
We've talked. I'm fine.
He brakes.
Look out.
I'm fine.

GAME PLAN

All set?
We can do this
We've got coaching
We've got attitude
We've got heart

The players know their positions
Buddy, Me and Mom
head to Boston
for the big game.

Dad stays behind to
keep the job
the money
the health insurance.
Driving five hours on weekends
called in
as relief pitcher.

No home-field advantage.

Go Team.

LIST

1. Poker
2. Pitch
3. Spanish
4. Geometry
5. Harmonica

He's made a list
We've got a plan
Stuff he can learn

6. in a hospital bed
7. hooked up to IVs
8. and feeding tube
9. passing the days
10. preparing for what?

DIRECTIONS

Route 81 to the New York State Thruway
Stay on 90
through Albany
90 all the way
through Massachusetts
Exit 22
Tunnel to Prudential, out on Huntington
right on Longwood,
park on the right,
the hospital is directly across.

But do we know the way back home?

Children's Hospital

A giant giraffe
of plastic or papier-mâché
looming in the lobby.
A wall of fish
swimming beside the gift shop.
Brightly colored walls,
animal-wallpaper borders
and paw-print confetti carpeting.
A bright, welcoming place for children.
But in the mural beside the elevator
in tall teal and lime grass,
I spy a crouching lion.

VISITORS

Buddy's teacher, Mrs. Sheehan, has come
with a deck of Uno cards and one of the Harry
    Potters.
I put them with the two other decks and
the same six Potter books.

You know we've placed you with Mr. Morgans for
    next year.
I think you'll like having a male teacher for fifth
    grade.
Aziz Zughaib will be in your class too.
I imagine he has already told you.

Mrs. Sheehan is trying too hard
perched on the plastic chair.
Buddy is too tired to charm,
he nods a bit and closes his eyes.

Mom flits around
flashing me looks that say,
Please help, add something here.
I don't know what to say.

Mrs. Sheehan refocuses on Mom.
Talking, talking, talking — the two of them
a background of sound,
and odd laughter.

Buddy rubs my hand,
pleading with me to send his favorite
   teacher away.
What can I do but hold on tight, and fix his
   blanket?
The two of us short on energy, low on power.

Mrs. Sheehan waves and walks to the door,
Mom flutters behind,
*Buddy can you thank Mrs. Sheehan for coming all
   this way to see you?*
Buddy did you say thank you for the gifts?

Dugout/Dug in

We are four weeks into this
with no end in sight.
I am tired,
I am bored.
You are ungrateful
my mother tells me.

I miss Callie,
I miss swimming,
I miss the outdoors.

Is there still wind out there?
Is there something more than this controlled,
    air-conditioned, hygienic air to breathe?

I want to wear a tan,
I want to wear a sleeveless shirt,
I want to wear just a little too little for my
    mother's taste.

I want to eat a meal —
a real meal
with hot vegetables and no plastic cutlery.
I am sick of turkey sandwiches.
I am sick of Whoppers.

I know every inch of this hospital:
the gift shop, the cafeteria,
the linoleum and the sharp smell of plastic
and disinfectant.

I need to get out,
I am sick to death of this,
I am sick to death of me.

Beyond Room 5123

On days that Mom
takes time in the cafeteria
and Buddy sleeps,
I map all
the routes from home
to New York City.
I should probably figure out
the way from this hospital to
there but instead
I plan a better trip.
No Thruway for
Buddy and Me.
We'll take Route 81.
The TripTik mentions rolling hills,
but I know they're more than that.
Curving roads
around a bend
a new view of river and sky,
red and orange in Autumn,
impossible green until then.
Maybe we'll get off
and side-trip it
to Cooperstown.
Rt 20 and then 28
should take us right into town.

We'll wander as long as we like,
get lost in the Hall of Fame,
take some pictures,

buy some pricey souvenirs,
get back on the road.
Left on 23 and on to the Taconic
till we meet the Hutchinson Parkway
to the Bruckner and Major Deegan highways,
right on exit 5,
right again on 161st street,
and into the parking garage.
Buddy and me.
Dreaming our way
to Yankee Stadium.

Roster Change

First week of July means new Residents
   On Staff.
Fresh faces, fresh voices, fresh hope.
The word on 5 West
from the experienced parents:
Be careful.
These newly minted doctors
they don't know what they're doing yet.

Buddy and me we pay attention
during rounds.
I stay close to him and whisper:
Which one might have some good jokes?
Which one might be a grouch?
Which one is nervous around sick kids?

Mom pays attention
to their hand washing,
their note taking,
their questions,
their answers.
Watching for incompetence.

Five step in with their Supervising Physician.
One reminds Buddy of shortstop Derek Jeter,
One reminds him of that one we hated,
The one who pretended Buddy couldn't hear
couldn't understand, didn't care.

One reminds him of funny Dr. Susan
　　back home.
He'll have to see about the other two,
wait to give them nicknames only we will know.

But I've got a nickname I'll keep to myself
for Dr. Harkness, that Derek Jeter one,
and hope Mom doesn't find fault
with his questions, answers, note taking and
　　hand washing.

Summer Sun

Dr. Hotness is here
checking on Buddy's counts
talking to Mom,
high-fiving Buddy,
glancing at me.

I know he's too old,
probably married,
doesn't matter
a bit.

Looking feels like living
and he is here
slouching with that clipboard,
breathing the same
sanitized-for-Buddy's-protection
air.

Home Rules

The walls in this Ronald McDonald House are
  thick.
Such an old house of plaster
and pain.
The House that Love Built,
it's true.
Volunteers bring cakes, hot-chocolate packets,
new pillows, plastic toys, pans of scalloped
  potatoes
and hope.

Posted rules:
1. Clean up your own mess
2. Change your own sheets
3. Do your own laundry
4. Leave your room ready for the next family

Families come and go.
Some laughing, lingering
taking home children still in Thank God
  Remission.
Some leave quickly,
packing up fast,
not cleaning before they go.
Shooed out,
don't worry
we'll take care of it for you.

The walls in this Ronald McDonald House
    are thick
but everyone can hear
when the O'Hares leave for Maine,
without the one that brought them here.

MIA

Buddy's counts?
Not good.
Buddy's breathing?
Not good.
Buddy's color?
Gray.

Dr. Harkness?
Doesn't stop by anymore
to say:
Hello Slugger
We made you a BoSox fan yet?
Dr. Crane?
Doesn't stop by anymore
to say:
What's the good word?
You still rooting for those Yankees?

They check in
during rounds
staying just long enough
to check his chart, ask medical questions
and not quite look us in the eye.

DREAM

At night I creep onto
5 West
and into Buddy's room
and disconnect the tubes
the wires
the sensors.

I run
carrying Buddy in his old blue plaid baby
  blanket
five hours home to Dr. Delaney.

He knows a cure.
He's just figured it out.
He can keep my brother alive
with the magic of science, research, medicine.

All I have to do is get Buddy to Dr. Delaney
All I have to do is get Buddy to Dr. Delaney
All I have to do is get Buddy to Dr. Delaney

in my blue plaid dreams.

Numbers

Mom has to get away
just for 2 days.
Has to get back
to 4105 Barrow Road
to help Dad this 1 time.

Because water heaters break down at 3AM
and dogs need surgery before 4 on Saturdays,
even when there are other fires to fight.
So she leaves Friday at 6PM,
be back Sunday around 3PM.
I'm to hold down the fort on 5 West
and in Room 12 at the Ronald McDonald
    House.

What can happen in just 2 days' time?

COVER GIRL

Dr. Ice Queen
Asks me to step inside
The only room on this whole damn floor
Where the family can have some privacy.

Dr. Ice Queen
Has assembled a few nurses and their clipboards
In the only room on this whole damn floor
Where the family can have some privacy.

Dr. Ice Queen
Tells me they've called my parents and told
    them to come quick
In the only room on this whole damn floor
Where the family can have some privacy.

Dr. Ice Queen
Says that Buddy is Stage 4 and declining fast
In the only room on this whole damn floor
Where the family can have some privacy.

Dr. Ice Queen
Informs me that there is nothing more they
    can do
In the only room on this whole damn floor
Where the family can have some privacy.

Dr. Ice Queen picks up a magazine
From the laminate end table
And discusses the beauty of Isabella Rossellini
With the two nurses and their clipboards

Not looking at me again
Not talking to me again
Leaving me without a place
To tear, to scream, to cry alone

In the only room on this goddamn floor
Where the family can have some privacy.

VIGIL

Sitting in his room,
waiting for Mom and Dad,
not sure if he's sleeping or unconscious.
How do I know? Does it matter which now?
His nurse in and out, checking him, checking
     charts,
says we're keeping him
comfortable as she dims the lights again.
Then his right hand fingers move slow, then
     quick
he says something as I lean close
What ya doing little brother? Can I
get you something? I whisper, *Are you cold?*
I reach for his blanket, he mumbles something
his fingers busy again, one finger, no two,
and then I see he's flashing signs,
just like he taught me
calling for a fastball down the middle
telling me something
my ear to his chest
I'm calling the game, he says.

MY BROTHER

He left so quickly,
He left so much,
He left me.

POSTSEASON

September–November, Senior year

Dawn's Early Light

The alarm
breaks
my sleep
breaks
not quite
awake
not quite
an ache
reminds me
reminds me
reminds me

Oh God

Buddy dies each morning at 6:02.

PLACES

The kitchen is out-of-bounds,
we can't eat at the table
because of his chair.
Can't watch TV in the den because
a game might be on.
No one can enter his room
for fear of a massive breakdown.
So they stay in their room
and I in mine,
three of us parked somewhere
between numb and
devastation.

Time

Flipping through last year's yearbook
Callie asks
Any interest in going to the island Friday night?
Laura and Jill are going, Anthony and Rick too.
They've got a good band this week,
might do you good.
Why would she think it would do me any good?

That's the last place I want to be
around kids trying to sneak a drink,
listening to music so loud you can't talk
or think.
Not this time is all I answer.
I suppose she's just trying to help
but I don't have energy for fun.
Let's stay in then, sleep at my house
maybe rent a movie and eat too much.
What do you say, Kit?
She straightens the picture of Buddy on
    my desk.
Not this time is all I answer,
not this time, though I can't imagine
there will come a time.

School Starts Wednesday

I ought to get new jeans,
my clothes look old
and a little too big.
But that would take energy
and what I need is more sleep.

I ought to get notebooks
and filler paper,
my backpack still stuffed
with last year's locker remains.
But that would take time
and what I need is more sleep.

I ought to call Callie
compare our schedules,
teachers and plans,
ask if her homeroom is in the new wing.
But that would take interest
and what I need is more sleep,
just a little more sleep.

PHONE MESSAGE
FROM CALLIE

You gotta get out Kit. Meet me tonight at St. Bridget's.
I'm serving fish dinners to my unsuspecting fellow
Catholics from 5 to 6. And from 7 to 8, I'll be
maitre d' and can show you to a fine table overlooking
the gymnasium. Come on Kit Kat, meet me for a good
Catholic meal or we'll go bowling or something as
soon as I'm done.
Call me.

I replay the message
a couple times.
Not for the details — I won't be going,
but just to hear
the sound normal used to make.

MAKE IT STOP

I don't feel like going
don't want to see a movie
don't want to shop for shoes
don't want to look at her magazine
her nail polish, her new sweater
don't want to go for a hike
don't want to try a swim
don't want to tune up the bikes
the car, her guitar.
She's driving me crazy.

CALLIE AGAIN

She's got to stop asking me.
I don't want to talk.
Talking won't fix anything.
I need to be left alone.
So I tell her.

What I Wanted Him to Know

Maybe because Buddy was so much younger,
maybe because he was so agreeable,
I treated him like a guinea pig:
my own little school experiment,
teaching him things
I wanted him to know.

When Buddy was in second grade
I taught him fractions.
How to add them,
subtract them
and eventually
to multiply them.

I showed him how it was
all a game,
a puzzle to master,
the fun in the tracking
and tracing
of answers.

Mom was always good at numbers,
Dad not so.
But Buddy and I
were like our own math club,
a secret sibling society,
a team of two,
calculating.

Parental Pressure

I'm fine.
I'm fine; I am dealing with this just fine.
I don't need this,
I read Elisabeth Kübler-Ross
back in ninth grade for a research paper.

Okay, I'll go.
But I'm only doing this for you.

BGT (Bereavement Group for Teens)

We sit in the same chairs every week
as if they were assigned.
A smaller, quieter version of high school.
We've got a Save the Whales Girl here,
we've got a boy in black and chains, tats and
    piercings,
a guy wearing a scribbly concert T-shirt and
    a girl in way too much eye shadow.
I'm guessing the one in the corner is a jock,
and the one on the ratty love seat too.
We've got a couple of fidgety sisters and a new
    preppy girl,
We've got a way-too-cheery bereavement
    facilitator and we've got me.

Fidgety Sister #1 sits all crumpled up every
    week,
going through her box of tissues every week.
Save the Whales Girl has never said a word
and the Jock just nods and stretches a lot.

Let's open up a discussion on how we're getting by
    and if we've made plans to cope with the upcoming
    holidays and who wants to begin?

You'd think we were all in detention.
Nobody talks.

Then New Prep Girl begins and never ends
and you know,
you just know
that she sees BGT as another class to pass.
She uses all the Healing Phrases
gives us all suggestions,
and checks off her progress in all the stages
as if there was a way to do it right, get a good
    grade in Grief Work 101.

And if Callie and I still spoke the same language
    I'd tell her all about it.

AWAKENING

If only I'd known
to savor the days
of flannel sleep
to embrace the time
within the hollow, the nest.
If only I'd known
this was the best
I could ever
expect again.

Numb was a dear, sweet friend,
a warm soft bed,
a place to rest
the last of me.

TRIPLE A

I call and give them my member number
A gift from Mom when I got my license
Advance planning so I would be safe
Away.

I order a tour book and a TripTik for
A journey I won't be taking
A distraction to keep me from exploding
Apart.

I say Houston because it doesn't matter where
An exercise in sanity: tracing roads, imagining
    routes
A reason to get up in the morning
Again.

BECOMING CATCHER

Back when he was little, back before he was sick
I teased him that it was the accessories he
   wanted
like picking Malibu Barbie because she came
with surfboard, beach towel and shades,
that he knew he'd look cool
with his cap on backwards, a chest protector
   and shin guards.

Mom: *No. Too dangerous. Kids who don't know any*
better swinging bats wildly at your head kids who
don't know any better throwing pitches at your face
kids who don't know any better crashing into you
running home. Play first base. Pitch. Not catcher. No.

Buddy: *Yes. Please. Catcher's the smartest one out*
   there
I'll call the pitches, track the batters,
run the game
Let the pitchers get the glory, I can make the wins.

I steal his chest protector from his closet
And hide it in my own
I want to remember
the way he grinned the day
he brought it home
and I called him
Malibu Barbie.

Box Scores

She's always been obsessive
clean hands, clean house,
nothing overdue, nothing underdone
nothing undone.

My father and I, a team
forged by defying her orders
or at least meeting winks
behind her whirlwind back,
thrown together for a common cause,
kidding each other about her ways,
united in our not-her-ness.

Buddy was her teammate
hurrying behind,
wanting to please
rewarded with her light-up-the-town smile,
her pats on the back and trips to McD's,
on a mission, just the two of them,
clean, orderly, happy,
together.

Her time, her interest, her drive,
now spent online, on the phone, at the
    university library,
researching new theories, techniques.
Looking for answers,
wanting to know,
Why Buddy? Did I screw up during the pregnancy?

Did the lawn service, or the power lines
near the house back in Binghamton cause this?
Did the doctors mess up, ignore signs,
not order enough tests, not try the latest chemo, not
    try hard enough?

We don't play in the same league anymore.
She does not recognize us as the opposing team.
Doesn't ask anything of me,
Doesn't notice Dad's vacancy.
Doesn't bleach anything anymore.

The doctors are the opposing players,
the disease the game to be understood,
    vanquished, won.
But the game is long over
and we're all undone.

HALF

I see Aziz
turning the corner of Meadow onto Barrow
and I look for Buddy
coming along on his heels
the way these two always
complete each others' shadow
and then
I remember
Buddy is in the past tense.

TEAMMATE

Callie was with me
when I woke up
at 6 AM with my first period
at Maddie Cerio's eleventh birthday slumber
    party.
She told Maddie that I had a really bad
    stomachache and walked me home without
    waiting for a party favor.

Callie was with me
when I tripped over Marcus Delano's cello
right onstage as we filed
in for the Herald Junior High Spring Fling
    Concert.
She pulled me up and shielded me while I fixed
    my black swirly skirt and she said that nobody
    had even noticed.

Callie was with me
when Kyle Siebert dumped me
in front of his friends
in the hall by his locker on the way to gym class.
She guided me to the bathroom and skipped
    chemistry to mop up my mascara and make
    up new names for Kyle.

Callie was with me
during the calling hours
2 to 4 and 5 to 7,

Tuesday and Wednesday at Mender's
  Funeral Home.
She brought my parents paper cups of water
  and winced when she heard some people say
  that Buddy was in a better place now.

Callie was with them
when I noticed she never said Buddy's name
  anymore and
I screamed at our whole table, including her
  boyfriend, Rick,
in the cafeteria during fifth period lunch.
She said that I'm too sensitive and that they
  didn't want to say the wrong thing so they
just didn't say anything to me anymore.

Where is Callie now
that my stomach really hurts, and my clothes
  don't fit right,
and I must wear waterproof mascara?
Where is she now that I really need her to fix it
  all up?
Where is she now that I told her to go?

SENIORS

I have got the stupidest friends.
People who care only for talk of football games,
    college visits,
and SAT scores.
People who plan way too much and way too far
    ahead.

Don't they know it could all be over tomorrow?
What makes them think any of us will get
    through senior year
and on to college alive?

ANOTHER MEETING

The bereavement counselor
wants to know if we know
about them.
The seven stages of grief?
Seven stages?
Seven?
I know the truth.
There's one stage.
One goddamn stage.
One.

No Lifeguard on Duty

Save the Whales Girl has a sister,
can't be more than four or five,
bitty baby Eco-Child,
bitty baby grieving child.

Save the Whales Girl kissed that sister,
hugged her head and sent her in
to that room right next to our room,
BGT for kids.

Save the Whales Girl lost a sister
to her Grandma's swimming pool.
left the three as just two sisters,
left them paddling in this hall.

Save the Whales Girl has a sister,
way too young to be so old.
Now she knows that children die,
understands that she will die.

Save the Whales Girl lost two sisters,
one to water,
one too wise.

BGT Counsels

We should be careful
around each other.
We should be supportive
of each other's grief.
We should be closer
than ever
for what we've just gone through.

Then why does the sound
of my mother's
latest theory
make me want to scream?
Why does the sight
of my father
crying in the garage
make me want to run?

And why do they
leave me
so often
alone?

BETRAYAL

We never told him he might die.
We thought
a winning attitude
would carry him through,
would help him fight,
would make him all right.

Too fast
the coma came
too fast
to tell him
what might happen
too fast
to prepare him
if things didn't go well.
Too fast.

Is he up in heaven
angry
because a big sister
should have told?

Journeys

Back at the Triple A
Peppy Lady greets me
like an old friend.
I pick up this week's TripTik,
this time it's Tampa.
I flip the pages taking
me through the Mid-Atlantic states
and into Florida
until I pick out the way.
I-275 to US 92,
take exit 41B,
which used to be Old Route 23,
go approximately 3 miles,
turn left into Legends Field.
Oh yeah, Legends Field,
Buddy loved the name of
that Yankees' spring training camp.

You sure do travel a lot,
Peppy Lady interrupts my head trip
stuffing the TripTik
and Florida Travel Guide
into the plastic car trash bag
with the 800 emergency number
printed right there on it
just in case,

comforting the traveler
with the promise
of roadside assistance,
"Travel With Someone You Trust."

KITCHEN

I think
I'm hungry
then
it turns out
I'm not.

HOT STOVE

December–February

SEASON OF HOPE
AND TRADES

A couple of years ago Buddy couldn't believe
I'd never heard of it.
Everybody knows Hot Stove, Kit.
It's the off-season, when they make the trades.
Everybody knows? I didn't. My friends didn't.
I couldn't get past the phrase "Hot Stove"
I imagined a bunch of guys in pinstripes
flipping pancakes and frying bacon.
No way. It's like in the old-timey days,
Guys sitting around wood stoves
in those old stores like on TV.
But I didn't get what that had to do with
    baseball.
They talk about the year to come,
how their team is gonna win the pennant
on account of the trades.
He dragged out all his baseball books
the trivia, the encyclopedias
to make me understand
this season of hope and trades.
We could use more pitching, Kit
another reliever, one more closer.
He was all glow-y and earnest,
an evangelist
who thought that I would come around,
share his passion
if he could only provide me with enough facts.

I didn't have the time, the interest, the patience.
My resistance now
a regret I'd like to trade.

WE THREE

are all in different places
each in different moods.
Not wanting our own
to infect another
we steer clear.

WHAT IF I CRIED

and let go just a little,
stayed here in this
warm kitchen, actually ate something
sobbed if I needed to,
released some tension,
just for a night.
What if I cried
and let go just a little,
remembered myself, my old life,
wallowed a bit?
What if I cried
and let go just a little,
read a magazine,
soaked in the tub,
worried less about the future,
took care of just now.
What if I tried to defy my nature?
Would my parents pull themselves together or
would whatever is left of us fall all apart?
What if I cried, just for a night?

WORDS

I could write a new dictionary
a specific nobody-would-want-to-look-up-
    these-words
dictionary.
But if they did
they would find sob
moan
mourn
wail
rent
wretch.
They would find sorrow,
which is the word that holds them all:
the sore, the ohh, the owwwww.

CALLIE STOPS BY

*I've got my dad's Mustang. He hardly lets me sit in it,
let alone drive it. He thought we should go see a
movie or catch a bite, drive around town, or go to the
park. He even handed me money. Getting weird in his
old age.*
Come on.

For a moment I forget
and it's just us and the autumn air calling,
just us and that great car,
The Man Magnet,
we dubbed it
a million trillion years ago.

*Thanks, but I should really get my French done and
   my room cleaned*
and maybe start dinner.

I'm trying, she says. *I'm trying you know.*

I think I'm trying too
I think . . .
but right now
it's hard to tell.

Callie backs out.

Aziz

I've seen him riding his bike
back and forth in front of our house
pretending he's not really looking.
I've seen him hop off and check the chain
at the base of our driveway
acting real interested in the grease and
  the pedals.
He's there again now and
I know I should call out to him
invite him in
comfort him in some way.
He was Buddy's best friend
nearly another brother and I know
he's hurting.
But I can't take on
his pain too
and it would hurt too much
to have someone of Buddy's shape and size
inside this house,
sitting at the kitchen table
or over there by the stairs.
So I just wait and watch him
pedaling away again.

FLAMMABLE

Dad's mad again
He took my '97 Civic
to the touchless all-night car wash
and noticed the gauge sitting
on "E" again.

Can't you keep it filled?
Can't you be responsible?
Can't you plan ahead?

If he only knew
what I might do
with the clothes stashed
behind my jumper cables
beside the emergency road kit
beneath the red gym bag
with food
enough to last
twelve hundred miles or so.

Doesn't he know
the temptation at hand?
Better just put in ten again.
Danger is a full tank
of gasoline.

TESTING . . . 1, 2, 3 . . . TESTING

I put on that one
that kills her
cut so low
hardly a strap
the one I bought
last summer with Callie
from a stand at Bright's Beach.

I put on that one
even though
it's too cool
to wear it
to see what she'd do
to see if she'd notice
to see if she'd remember.

I put on that one
because the polka-dot pattern
should have woken her up
should have reminded her
that she's still
my mother.

Buddy's Bad Habits

1. Peeled his nails
low and raw
fingertips sore
and often bleeding

2. Terrible singing voice
loud and flat
mixed up tunes
confused lyrics

3. Wounded the bathroom
when he took showers
capless shampoo, dripping bath mat
puddles beside the tub

4. Wanted a gerbil
then neglected her cage
Mom threatened
to call the Humane Association or give it away

I'm just going to rub against all that
for a while
to keep him here, to keep him real
so he doesn't turn into some
perfect shadow of a skinny nine-year-old,
some polished-up memory
angel boy.

Because it's easier to remember that Buddy
1. always shared his fun-sized bag of M&M's
2. knew a million jokes
3. could find lost keys, missing glasses, and my homework
4. loved that Winn-Dixie book
5. quoted *The Phantom Tollbooth* like he wrote it himself
6. cried with Aziz when their bandaged sparrow died
7. thought I was Einstein helping him with his math homework

I've lost my little brother,
my biggest fan.
What if I lose the dirty details, the messy memories,
the incredible sound of his voice?

3:46 AM, DECEMBER 18

Play a game
that you've invented
against the Internet
and all those mapping Web sites.
How far is it to Tupelo?
and what about Beloit?
Wager yourself
then plug in the numbers.
See how close you get
then compare and compete
with the next site.

You'll eat up plenty of time
and miles
driving in your desk chair.

Missing Man Formation

It's like Dad's left us too.
It's like he's just checked out.
It's like he's a shadow
of who he used to be.

I see him eat sometimes,
bowls of cereal
cups of coffee
once a slice of banana bread
brought over by the neighbor who knows
we're not over it yet.

I know he sleeps here
but mostly he just leaves here.

If we pass at breakfast or at bedtime
he asks if school is okay,
he asks if Group is okay,
he asks if I need anything.
His eyes beg me to say "no"
And I do.

JUNIOR PROM PICTURES

The one with me and my date
taken by the photographer in the hall
beneath tulle and tiny lights.
Mark Simone, poor guy.
I cared more about my dress
than who I would go with.

The one my mom took
of me and Mark, Callie and Rick
in the backyard shivering beside Dad's snow-
    covered roses.
Callie looking like she goes to a prom
every Saturday night,
the guys looking a little scared.

The one of just me in my bedroom
my hair the way I had to have it,
just like the magazine,
looking like some other nervous girl in blue
    satin.

The one Callie took of the family
that same prom night.
My dress twisted,
all of us scrunched,
Buddy rabbit-earing me,
Dad's arm around Mom's shoulders,
all of us saying "cheese."

One week before
diagnosis day,
I look closely at Buddy
trying to see the secret he's hiding
in his grin and his freckles and his rabbit-ear
    fingers.
The secret that will blow us all apart
one week after the night
of pictures beside Dad's roses
waiting to bloom.

Bombs Bursting in Air

Who is she over there by the refrigerator?
This woman screaming at my father,
this woman banging cupboards and doors,
this woman throwing napkins on the floor,
that woman doesn't resemble my mother at all.

THOSE GIRLS

We are not friends
they've just taken
an interest in me
looking for a fix
don't I recognize this.

I know this little group
AshleyBrittanyCourtneyJennifer
I remember them well,
back in sixth grade
and our first middle school dance
all of us there thinking we were
so grown up
so high school.

They were the ones
forever running in and out
of the girls' bathroom
laughing, crying
craving catastrophe,
Brittany likes Danny but he likes Ashley, Omigod
the stars of their own dramas
creating tragedy.

Now they want a bit of me,
to reflect my sorrow,
to absorb the attention
they believe is around here somewhere.

But I'm not supplying whatever it is they're
  buying,
these drama addicts
better move along.

WHAT WILL WE DO WITH HIS STUFF?

Maybe give Aziz a few special things
his baseball cards, his chess set,
guard the rest with our pain.
But what about his backpack filled with
school papers?
What about the Happy Meal toys
he hadn't parted with yet?
His old certificates from camp
proclaiming him
"Most Improved Swimmer" and "Sweetest
    Smile"?
What will we do with the clothes, the curtains,
    the closet?
I can see from the door
he's got junk crammed beneath his bed.
What will we do with the trash
in the Einstein wastebasket
beside his desk?
What will we do?
Close the door again,
close the door.

MY ROOM

Sort through clothes
and fill bags for the Rescue Mission,
attack the desk,
and the trunk at the foot of my bed.
Do I really need the dolls on the high shelf?
or the little boxes on the dresser?
Clear the closet quickly
of old sports equipment
and hats I never wear.
Out, out, out,
bag after bag.
What do I really need?
Out, out, out,
and then
breathe
a little easier.

Harbor Call

Out back the snow is heaped on
terra-cotta crocks holding
geranium skeletons,
the grass long and matted
beneath snowdrifts,
the garden hose in a
tangle along the fence,
Dad's roses untrimmed and uncovered beside.

Those dishes in the sink
smell of sour milk and
pepperoni.
Someone should wipe the floor
in front of the fridge
and clear the kitchen counter of mail,
paper plates, coffee cups and
sympathy cards.

At first it was relief
not having them on me
about chores, schoolwork, clothes.
But my sure thing A+ in French
isn't even a sure B anymore,
and I'm getting tired of scooting out at the bell
avoiding Madame's concerned looks and
offers of help.

At first it was relief
both too worn, both too empty.
All of us islands
too distant to matter.
But the weight of it all calls me to water.
Something must be done around here.
Something must be done around here.
Do something
Row.

SCAR TISSUE

Soaking in my tub
I notice
the ring of caulk blackened in the corners,
beneath the soap dish too
a scabbed wound of mildew.

I pick at it with fingers
and a rattail comb,
pulling out bits of crumbly scum and sealant
laying it along the side of the tub,
leaving a gaping one-inch slash.

Toweling off
I grab tweezers from the drawer,
and pull out more dark, stiff caulk.
Another couple inches of crevice revealed
where tile used to meet tub.

Focused I dig,
pull, scrape out
diseased scar tissue,
wiping with a washcloth
opening the wound to light and air.

Soon I'll find my bathrobe,
get a screwdriver,
finish it right.
But for now I'll continue with comb and
    tweezers

completing the crevice, digging out
   the contamination

undressed and undeterred.

SPRING TRAINING

February–March

BATTING PRACTICE

Christmas?
the 4th of July?
his birthday, November 23rd?
his death day, August 15th?
Which should be
the hardest day?

Not this day:
they showed it on the news,
blue sky, white cloud
pinstripes
on deep green grass.
I feel Buddy's old excitement
on the breeze
a faint dirt and earthworm scent
a quickening breath
an expectation
of hope.

Spring training has begun
and I just want to tear that southern
   ballpark down.

Hardware

I would have thought
the 24-hour grocery store would have had
towel rods, toilet paper holders, caulk.
But all they had were shower curtain rings
and those sticky fish and flower decals and mats
   for tubs.
The pimply boy I recognized from school,
but couldn't tell you his name stocking
   lightbulbs said
You need to go to a hardware store for that
the one in the village will have that stuff.
I didn't know we had one in the village.
Right near the bowling alley. You know. The
   hardware store.
I guess I'd never noticed that low building,
   peaked roof, big lit-up sign
right there in the center of town.
Funny how you don't see what's always been
   right there
until you need it.

INSTALLING A TOWEL ROD

I know the difference now

In his hardly there
stumbling around
saggy-blue sweatpants and
Rochester Red Wings faded T-shirt
Dad pulled together an answer
to the question I needed most
What's a Philips head screwdriver?

He showed me the little plus-sign
end and compared it to a flathead
looking at me like he hadn't realized I still
   lived here
not interested enough to ask why
I needed to know.

HOME REPAIRS

The old guy at the Village Ace Hardware
showed me the Red Devil caulk-removing tool
when I bought the stretchable, mildew-resistant
   tube of bright white caulk.

Next time, use this, Missy.
It'll be easier to get the old caulk outta there.

I used it Saturday
when I went after the caulk
around the kitchen sink.

The right tool for the right job,
You've heard that one, Missy?

I went back to that old guy,
Mr. Larkin,
and asked about grout.

Piece of cake there, Missy.
Let me show you how.

I regrouted the tiles
in my parent's shower
and then applied the smoothest bead of caulk.

Mr. Larkin showed me how
to cut molding with a miter box and saw
just in case I ever needed to know.

Measure twice, cut once
Missy, I bet you'd have done that anyway.

The day I accepted a part-time job
with the Village Ace Hardware
my boss, Mr. Larkin, printed up a name badge
   for me.

I told him to put my new name on it,
my competent, unbroken,
name for just here on it,
my nobody-in-this-store-knows-my-little-
   brother-died
name on it.
I told him to put "Missy" on it.

THE WINDUP

I ring up replacement toilet parts,
boxes of assorted screws, furnace filters,
seed packets and peat pots.

I walk people to the aisle where we keep tubes
of stretchable, mildew-resistant bright white
   caulk
and tell them how to apply it.

I hand them a Red Devil caulk-removing tool
and wish them well, knowing
that this simple act of removing old, decayed
   caulk
and replacing it with a clean, fresh bead
of stretchable, mildew-resistant bright white
   caulk
might restore more
than just their bathroom.

I explain how to fix a leaky toilet with a fresh
$2.79 beeswax ring, how to prime molding and
which oil paint will cover like glass.

I am able somehow
to find my smile
to feel like my old self
No. Like a new and improved self
No. A sadder yet more complete self
at the Village Ace Hardware.

Curve Ball

Wednesday my car was in for a tune-up,
my father walked in at eight-thirty to pick
   me up,
saw me talking, nodding, laughing with
   customers,
saw my name badge.
His stare told me he thought
I'd betrayed us all.
Not missing Buddy enough if I can smile over
   the 9-inch roller covers
and 3-ply plastic dropcloths.
Some girl named Missy meant he was childless
   after all.

DESIGNATED HITTER

Dad hasn't been in the rotation
hardly talked
hardly showered.

The day he came back to us
he tripped over Buddy's mitt
his catcher's mask
and the stiff shin guards
piled by the back garage door.

That was the day he started talking again
That was the day he started seeing again
That was the day he came back to us,
grabbed up Buddy's baseball bat
and smashed down the backyard fence.

Break Down

That customer didn't expect the story of my life
ringing up his lightbulbs and furnace filter.
All he did was ask
how I was doing
this fine day.
He got the condensed Buddy-died-in-August
    story,
don't-know-if-mom-and-dad-will-get-through-
    this story,
me-I'm-doing-okay story,

Except I never stopped.

Somehow sitting on Mr. Larkin's tippy, torn
    swivel chair
in the back room, clasping a wad of tissues,
Gary, the Guy Who Repairs Screens and
    Cuts Wood,
not sure where to look,
eating his sandwich in two bites and bolting
    back to the floor.

Mr. Larkin steady and nodding and waiting
    while I
cry like I had days to do it,
cry like I hadn't done it before,
cry because nine-year-old catchers
    shouldn't die.

AT THE VILLAGE ACE HARDWARE

Mr. Larkin and I pack boxes
with rollers, brushes
electrical outlets, switch plates
and most of aisle five.
Donations for the Homes of Hope
project on Lock Street.
He has another box
on the floor between us,
looks like cookies and M&M's in there.
Gotta take care of the folks taking care, Missy.
Those volunteers are giving up their free time
to renovate those houses,
making life better for a couple families in need.
We screech the packing tape around
some filled boxes.
You need any time off Missy, you let me know.
Mr. Larkin tosses my favorite, black licorice,
into the goodies box, tapes it shut
and winks.

ON LOCK STREET

A gray one, a white one
next door,
two-story, nearly identical
Homes of Hope.
Signs, shingles, wood scraps,
cluttering the front yards,
hammering, whistling
something dropping, crashing
a holler, a laugh
and Save the Whales Girl dragging
a two-by-four out the front door
of the white one.

THE GRAY ONE

I'm assigned to the painting crew
calling themselves "Holy Rollers,"
a couple of retired church guys,
husband-and-wife hairdressers
and a quiet father of four.

Together we tackle
the kitchen just left
by the cupboards and counters team.
The trim cutters clear out
as we start wiping sawdust,
Sheetrock and plaster dust away
the church guys showing me how.

Prepping and taping
they draw me in fast,
unpardonable puns
and wisecracks flying,
the hairdressers insisting
I give as good as I get.
Stirring, pouring, cutting, rolling
gallons of color,
brushstrokes on trim.

Funnier than I'd figured,
swearing more than they ought,
these paint-spattered church folks
aggressively friendly,

perspiring, praising, painting,
reminding me how I used to feel
among friends.

NAMES

A week later
on the same crew
Holy Rollers in the foyer,
just us two
painting the back bedroom blue.
Save the Whales Girl wields
her roller while I'm cutting in
on a ladder, at the ceiling,
careful not to mar the white.
We work in silence
and then some talking
about our schools,
about our group,
about our families and our missing one.

Kit, why does everyone here call you Missy?
How do I explain?
Well, I got this job . . . and they didn't know about
  Buddy, about me . . .
and I . . . I see her nod
and I know she knows.
Save the Whales Girl
had a sister,
Save the Whales Girl
has a friend,
Save the Whales Girl
has a name,
Lydia.

CALLIE

I call her
because I miss her
and I miss the me I was with her.

Answering Machine #1

How do you leave a message
that says
you are my best friend,
you are my lifeline,
you should call me right back?

You don't.

Answering Machine #2

I plan what I'll say when
the machine picks up
so I don't blow it
again.
I rehearse a message,
a tone of voice,
and dial
mouthing silently
my message of reconciliation
as the ringing begins.
But then,
Callie picks up
and I have the wrong message ready
so I stumble through
Hello
and try to say *I've missed you.*
Callie just laughs
and says
I'm coming right over Kit Kat,
I thought you'd never call.

Sorrys All Around

Can you forgive me?
What's to forgive?
Have you missed me?
Don't you know that by now?
How will we ever catch up?
How could we not?

Energized by tears,
exhausted by laughter,
we hug, we hold, we hope.

A Player to Be Named Later

Sweeping
up sawdust,
teenage son
of the Holy Rollers hairdressers,
broom tucked in
close to his body
and slightly behind,
sweeping forward
from beside his right foot,
you can't not notice that
cute butt
in those perfect jeans,
those flexed arms,
in his sleeveless T-shirt,
bristles shush, shush, shushing
my face flush, flush, flushing
blood rush, rush, rushing
watching him work.

Lunch

The church
dropped off some
ham sandwiches and chips,
cokes and double fudge brownies
in what will be the living room eventually
Lydia and I eat with Mike, his name is Mike,
Cutest-Butt-Gorgeous-Arms-Hairdressers' Son,
   Mike.
I worry that I am giggling; I know that I am
   laughing too much
He must think I'm some ham-sandwich-eating-
   chip-chewing-giggling idiot.
Lydia winks at me and now I'm afraid to look at
her just in case I start blushing along with this
god-forsaken giggling and I wonder if he might
possibly go with me to the party
we'll have when we give the new homeowners
their keys and celebrate the completion of
another Homes of Hope restoration when he
leans forward and asks that very question
to me.

Mom Says

She's flying to San Antonio
to consult with a specialist
on Buddy's type of cancer.
Mom says
This is the last doctor
I'll need to see,
the last questions
I'll need to ask,
Mom says
I'll have some answers
after this.

But she said that before she left for Seattle
and before she wrote
to the Mayo Clinic and Sloan Kettering.
And there's a new
stack of medical journals
on what used to be her drafting table,
its jaunty angle flat
these past six months
at least.
Mom says
We'll finally know
as she packs
toothpaste
and her worn notebook,
Mom says
This is it.

Mom says.

Sneaking Around

I tell my parents I'm staying
with Callie
just to buy some time.
I beg Callie to tell them
I'm in the shower
or walking her dog
and I'll call right back
if they call for me.
Finally, I take Callie's cell
so I can get away
with it all.

URGE

I gas up and hit the Thruway
adrenaline and music take me
through Amsterdam and Schenectady.
Lunch gets me to the Massachusetts line,
their governor welcomes me
on a sign going by at 70.
Most of Massachusetts falls away
as the miles fly by
and I exit deep into Boston
and park in that same old lot.

Months have melted and it seems I've
not been gone long,
the murals, the wallpaper and papier-mâché
still on guard.
I ride the elevator to the fifth floor
and only then wonder
what kind of masochist am I
to come back to this place of failure,
to the last days of Buddy,
to this place that I hate.

But I push through the double doors
and walk past the glass-fronted rooms
that were not ours
to the one that was.
I know not to go into this empty room,
know not to compromise this waiting, clean
   space.

I just stand and look at what was once
Buddy's bed, Buddy's bulletin board,
Buddy's shelves and Buddy's window.
All empty now.
He's really gone.

Others have certainly occupied this room since
we hoped and suffered here.
But I don't want to think of them,
I have what I came for.

RELEASE

The way home
is much longer,
the radio doesn't know my tastes
this far from home.
I search for stations
through Lee and Chicopee,
get a meal, a bathroom break, a cup of tea
and five hours later pull into Callie's driveway.
I should feel guilty
I suppose, for lying and driving,
but instead I feel
a calm, a quiet, a peace.

SPACKLED

I'm put on roller detail
spreading sage over primer white.
These repaired walls
look perfect when you step back
so new, so clean.
Up close
slim scars remain,
filled cracks,
spiderweb veins,
trace trauma
and years of settling.
I can see it's good enough,
this house given
another chance,
redeemed by laughing,
sweating,
cussing care.

Home of the Brave

Holy Rollers have asked and
maybe I'll go with them.
Two weeks of painting houses
for their summer
Kentucky mission project.
Lydia says she'll go if I'll go,
neither of us needing to get ready
to go off to college come fall,
all of that planning, applying, accepting
coming at a time
we were barely breathing.
Community college will do just fine,
no need to shop or pack
to enroll
in August or September.
So maybe a trip
south this summer,
south for a Homes of Hope Blitz,
south for a little more repairing,
will be just the right direction for me.

Catching Up

The night seems to have
no temperature at all
Callie and I squeak swaying
on her old backyard swing set
eating strawberries from a
travel mug
Callie holds low.

Graduation's in a couple months
How can it be so soon?
Seems like it all sped up
after elementary school was through.

I tell her about Mike,
squeak, squeak, she
tells me she's breaking up with Rick,
squeak, squeak.

More talk about everything and nothing, then
Callie drops the empty mug and pushes for
   the sky
pumping her legs, leaning way back
creaking the chain, soaring.
I push off
and fly beside her.

Feels like old times
every once and a while,
feels like new times
all the rest.
We'll manage.

In Buddy's Room

We've brought the tissues with us.
Dad and I sort through
Buddy's backpack and desk.
Mom peeks in, tries to help, leaves,
comes back to say,
Don't throw anything out.
Dad nods, squeezes her hand,
hands her *The Phantom Tollbooth*.
She clutches it, smiles, cries.
And that's how it goes, over and over.
We come, we cry, we leave,
we come.

Memorial Service, Putnam Park

Buddy's team stretches out along
the first base line,
black armbands
on red sleeves.
They're taller,
these friends of Buddy's.
Aziz and Ryan wave to me
then quickly look away.

Along the third base line,
the opposing team
a wiggling stretch
of green and white anxious
to get this game going.

My parents stand with Coach Manz
beside an evergreen, beside a hole.
Buddy always gave 110% Coach Manz begins.
Buddy would have laughed at that,
his little math mind disapproving of typical
    athlete talk.
*He was an accomplished catcher, a quick thinker and
    a good sport.*
Buddy was the heart of our team and we miss him.
We dedicate this tree in his memory.

The tree is settled down,
the dirt is heaped upon,
and right now I love Buddy's old coach,
his silly friends,
his sacred game.

Play Ball

the Umpire calls
from behind home plate,
and then
the sky opens.
A downpour scattering
everyone snatching up lawn chairs,
grabbing children,
racing to their cars.
My parents call out
We'll meet you back home.

I wait in the Civic
until everyone's gone,
until the downpour on my windshield
eases into a slow steady shower,
then head toward Buddy's home,
the plate where he crouched
surveying his field,
calling his game,
living his nine-year-old dream.
From this bent knee position
I see not just that Buddy died
but that he lived.

They grabbed up all the bases
in their hurry from the rain,
but they left behind home plate,
just for me I guess.

Home plate, that triangle atop a square,
It's shaped like every child's drawing,
the kind with a sun in the corner,
a tree and some flowers,
Everyone's home.

I pull it from the ground
and turn that rubber house around
as the rain nourishes
the tree
the field
and me.

Acknowledgments

Many thanks to Alvina Ling, and her assistant, Rebekah Mckay, on the Little, Brown end of my phone line. For a time they convinced me that none of my requests or questions were odd, and really none of their authors knew such things. I thank you both for your wisdom, your kindness, your patience.

Thank you to Ginger Knowlton for crying *again* on the train and telling me we'd sell it.

Thanks to the Vermont College MFA program and the faculty who encouraged me to "swing away," especially Kathi Appelt, Mel Glenn, Norma Fox Mazer and Alison McGhee. The VC students, especially the Salon, My Carmen and Evil Twin, all of whom safeguarded my sanity, deserve thanks and chocolate.

My critique group sisters have heard some of these poems way too many times and should be thanked for politely replying to my "This time I took the 'the' out; big difference, right?" with insight and endurance.

For the baseball double checks, thanks Dad, thanks Alex. To BJ Norrix and Armand Cianciosi, I think you'll see your parts as they go by.

And finally to my family—my Spackle—who knew I needed to tackle this subject one more time, in an attempt to honor and understand the experiences of too many bereaved children and parents whom we've come to know: I thank you and love you.